For anyone having a bad day,
that they may turn it around.
—C.B.C.

To Liam and Aya,
for all deeds and things broken, spilled, torn, lost, scattered,
forgotten, and ruined that made me momentarily ANGRY.
—H.K.

RODALE KiDS

An imprint of Rodale Books
733 Third Avenue, New York, NY 10017
Visit us online at RodaleKids.com.

Text © 2018 by Courtney Carbone
Illustrations © 2018 by Hilli Kushnir

Rodale Kids books may be purchased for business or promotional use
or for special sales. For information, please e-mail: RodaleKids@Rodale.com.

Printed in China
Manufactured by RRD Asia 201805

Design by Jeff Shake
Text set in Report School
The artwork for this book was created with pencil and paper,
then painted digitally in Adobe Photoshop.

Library of Congress Cataloging-in-Publication Data is on file with the publisher.

ISBN 978-1-63565-071-6 paperback
ISBN 978-1-63565-072-3 hardcover

Distributed to the trade by Macmillan
10 9 8 7 6 5 4 3 2 1 paperback
10 9 8 7 6 5 4 3 2 1 hardcover

This Makes Me Angry

BEEP! BEEP! BEEP!
My alarm clock goes off.
It sounds like yelling.
I want to yell back.

My little brother, Jack,
bursts into my room.
He wants to play.
I want to sleep.

I go into the bathroom.
Jack made a huge mess!

I feel heat rising
inside of me.
It is not just
from the shower.

Dad makes pancakes
for breakfast.
I like the crispy ones,
but Jack eats them all!

Mom's tea kettle is
boiling hot.
My insides are
boiling, too.

We get to school.
My teacher asks
for our homework.
I pull mine out.

Oh no!
My paper is covered
in crayon.
It is all Jack's fault.

I have to do the work
all over again!

My chest feels tight.
It stays that way
all morning.

Soon it is lunchtime.
I can't get my milk open.
I feel like I am going
to explode.

I rip the carton open.
It goes everywhere!

My friends laugh.
They think
it is funny.

I try to stay calm.
It does not work.
I yell at them instead.

A teacher sends me
to the principal.
Now I feel awful.

My face is hot.
My clothes are sticky.
I just want to go home.

The principal asks
what happened.

I start to cry.
I tell her everything.
She listens calmly.

The principal hands me
a small notebook.

She tells me
I can use the book
to draw how I feel.

21

I think about
all the bad things
that happened today.

I take a deep breath.
I draw everything
I feel in the book.

The pictures are
actually kind of funny.
I am not as angry now.

I go back to class.
I see the kids
from lunch.

I tell them I am sorry.
They apologize, too.
I feel a lot better.

I tell my family
about the book
when I get home.

Jack wants to draw, too.
I give him the book.
He starts to scribble
on my drawings.

Jack draws a picture
of us holding hands.
I give him a hug.
All my anger melts away.

Today started out
as a bad day.
But it turned into
a very good one.

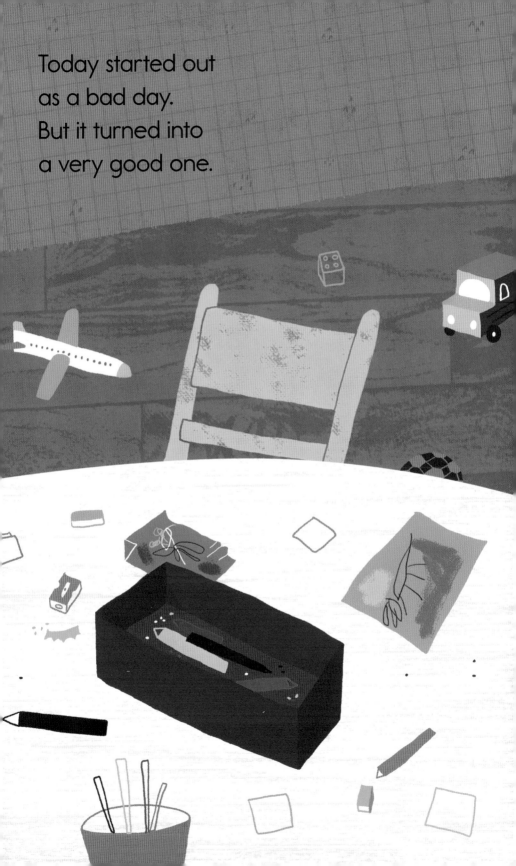

I was very angry
at times today.

What makes **YOU** angry?

Also available:

 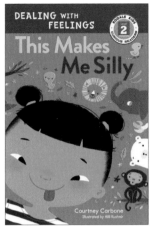 

Look for these other titles in the
DEALING WITH FEELINGS series:

- **This Makes Me Sad**
- **This Makes Me Silly**
- **This Makes Me Happy**
- **This Makes Me Scared**
- **This Makes Me Jealous**

To learn more about Rodale Kids Curious Readers,
please visit RodaleKids.com.